The Genie
in the Bottle

Retold by Rosie Dickins

Illustrated by Sara Rojo

Reading consultant: Alison Kelly
Roehampton University

This story is about a
fisherman,

a bottle

and a BIG
bad genie.

3

Once upon a time, a
fisherman went fishing.

He threw his nets again
and again.

He caught
slimy seaweed...

shiny shells...

and a smelly sock.

Then, he caught
something else.
"A fish!"
he cried.

But it wasn't.
It was an old bottle.

9

He pulled out the
stopper and looked in.

10

"Empty," he sighed.
And he threw it away.

CLUNK!

Suddenly, smoke poured
out. The smoke turned
into a huge face.

12

"Help," cried the
fisherman. "A genie!"

The genie's tummy
rumbled.

"I'm hungry," he growled.
"I'm going to EAT you!"

Meow!

"That's not very kind," said the fisherman.

"I'm hungry," shouted
the genie. "I've been in
that bottle for a long,
long time."

The fisherman
thought fast.

I have to
get him back
in the bottle.

"You were *inside* this bottle?" he asked.

"YES," snapped the genie.

19

The fisherman laughed.
"You'd never fit," he said.
"Watch," said the genie.

Whoosh

He whooshed back in...

...and the fisherman
pushed the stopper
in hard.

Then the fisherman
went on fishing...

Purrrr

...and caught a tasty
fish for dinner.

23

PUZZLES

Puzzle 1

Can you spot all the things
the fisherman caught?

seaweed   shells   sock
bottle   fish

Puzzle 2

Which sound goes where?

A
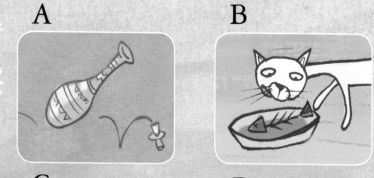

B

C
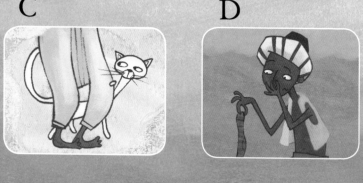

D

Yuck!

Meow!

Purrrr

CLUNK!

Puzzle 3

Put these pictures in order.

A

B

C

D

Puzzle 4
Spot the five differences between these two pictures.

Answers to puzzles

Puzzle 1

bottle

fish

sock

seaweed

shells

Puzzle 2

A — Clunk!

B — Purrrr

C — Meow!

D — Yuck!

Puzzle 3

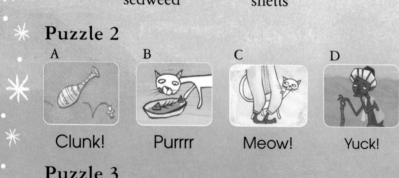

1. B
2. D
3. A
4. C

About the story

"The Genie in the Bottle" comes from a very old collection of stories known as *The Arabian Nights*. People say the stories were invented to entertain the King of Persia, by his clever and beautiful wife.

Designed by Michelle Lawrence
Series designer: Russell Punter
Series editor: Lesley Sims

First published in 2009 by Usborne Publishing Ltd., Usborne House,
83-85 Saffron Hill, London EC1N 8RT, England. www.usborne.com
Copyright © 2009 Usborne Publishing Ltd.